For Ben and Tom,
with thanks to Neil and Mum
— JR

For Milo, with love
— JM

International Standard Book Number: 1-56148-468-7

Library of Congress Catalog Card Number: 2004010873

Text copyright © Julia Rawlinson 2005 • Illustrations copyright © Jane Massey 2005

Original edition published in English by Little Tiger Press,
an imprint of Magi Publications, London, England, 2005.

Printed in Belgium by Proost NV.

Library of Congress Cataloging-in-Publication Data
Rawlinson, Julia.
Fred and the little egg / by Julia Rawlinson and Jane Massey.
p. cm.
Summary: After watching the swans by the lake care for their eggs, little bear Fred finds and builds a nest for an acorn, until Mommy
tells him of a better way to bring it to life.
ISBN 1-56148-468-7 (hardcover)
[1. Bears--Fiction. 2. Animals--Fiction.] I. Massey, Jane, 1967– ill. II. Title.
PZ7.R1974Fr 2005
[E]--dc22
2004010873

Fred and the Little Egg

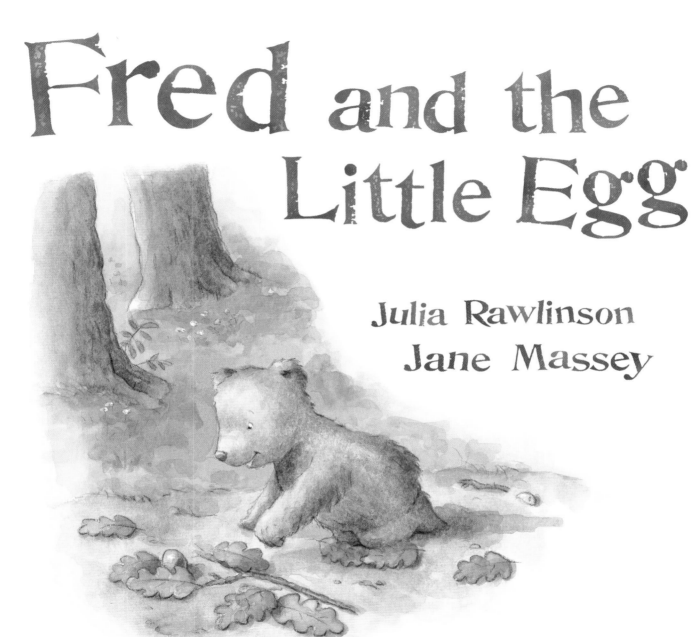

Julia Rawlinson

Jane Massey

Intercourse, PA 17534
800/762-7171
www.goodbks.com

Swans were nesting on the lake
near the den. Fred hid in the
reeds and watched them.

They built soft nests of sticks and moss
and laid large, white eggs in them.
Fred wanted to hatch an egg, too, so
he trotted home to the den.

"How do I make an egg?" asked Fred.

"Bears have cubs, not eggs," said Mommy.

"Then what can I put in my nest?" asked Fred.

"Bears have dens, not nests," said Mommy.

Fred still wanted to hatch an egg.
He wondered if he could borrow one.
He trotted back down the hill to the lake
and splish-splashed over to ask a swan.
The swan hissed fiercely as he came close.
Fred jump-bump-splish-splashed
backwards.

He picked himself up, shook the water from his fur, and squished back to the shore.

"I wasn't going to hurt it," he grumbled, stomping up the hill. "I'd have cared for it just as well as a swan." He plodded into the woods. Among the leaves, a shiny acorn suddenly caught his eye.

"A teeny weeny brown egg," thought Fred, "but who is here to hatch it?"

There was no one
hidden behind the trees.
Fred began to hope. Nobody
answered when he called. He gave
an excited squeak. He smelled only
flowers on the breeze and hugged himself
with happiness. The little brown egg was all
alone and needed him to care for it.

"I'll build you a beautiful nest," said Fred, as he carried the acorn to the lake. He built a nest of sticks and moss and settled the acorn into it.

He very carefully climbed on top and CRICK! CRACK! SPLASH! went the nest. Fred landed with a squish in the cold, wet mud with the acorn squashed underneath him.

"Are you all right, Little Egg?" asked Fred,
scrabbling in the mud. He gently
scooped up the acorn and
cradled it in his paws.

"I'll build you a warmer nest," said Fred,
trotting to a sunny hollow. He built
a nest of grass and flowers and
settled the acorn into it.

He very carefully climbed
on top and CHITTER!
CHITTER! CHATTER!
went a squirrel.

"I won't let anybody eat my egg," said
Fred with his fiercest stare.
   "Bears don't have eggs," said the squirrel,
poking at Fred's nest.
   "This bear does," said Fred firmly, giving
his rumbliest growl. The squirrel jumped,
waved his tail, and scurried crossly away.

With a
bounce-bounce-bump,
a baby rabbit tumbled into
the hollow.

"Do you want to come and
chase butterflies?" she asked,
brushing earth from her ears.

"Sorry, I'm busy," said Fred
importantly. "I have to hatch
my egg."

"Bears don't have eggs," said
the rabbit, peering at Fred's
nest.

"This bear does," said Fred
proudly, "and so I have to
hatch it."

With a
skitter-skitter-skip, a little
deer skidded down to
join them.

"Do you want to come and
jump sunbeams?" she asked,
shaking flowers from her fur.

"I do, but he's busy," said the
rabbit. "He has to hatch his egg."

"Bears don't have eggs," said
the deer, nibbling at Fred's nest.

"This bear does," said the
rabbit knowingly, "and so he
has to hatch it."

The deer and the rabbit skitter-bounced away,
but Fred sat still among the flowers.

He sat and he sat as the
sun rose high and the hollow
grew hotter and hotter.

He sat and he sat as
lunchtime passed and his
tummy began to rumble.

He sat and he sat through
the sleepy afternoon with
insects buzzing around him.

He sat and he sat
until the sun began to set and
his tummy was rumblier than thunder.
Then he picked up the acorn and carried it
gently all the way back to the den.

"My little brown egg won't hatch," said Fred,
feeling very tired and grumpy.
    "That won't hatch into a bird; it will grow into
a tree, like that tall, old oak," said Mommy.
    "If a tree hatched under me, I'd bounce
up to the clouds," said Fred. He
put down the acorn quickly.

"You don't have to sit on it; you just
have to plant it in the earth, like this,"
said Mommy.

"So I just sit here and wait?" asked Fred.

"It will take a long time," said Mommy.

"I've got nothing else to do until dinner."

"A very long time," said Mommy.

"Longer than dinnertime? What
about bedtime?"

"Much, much longer,"
said Mommy.

Fred didn't think he could sit still for
that long, so he looked at the earth
thoughtfully.
   "Will my egg be all right if I leave it?"
   "It will be safe down there,"
said Mommy.

"What if it gets lonely without me?"

"Worms will tell it stories," said Mommy.

"I'll miss you, Little Brown Egg," said
Fred. "I'll visit you every day."

"You'll soon have a little green
tree," said Mommy.

The little brown egg was silent.

So Fred padded off to
the tall, old oak, which rustled
its leaves in welcome. He climbed
into the branches and looked
down at the lake where the swans
were sitting quietly.

"I'm glad I don't have to sit on
my egg," said Fred, swaying happily.

Far below him, safe in the earth,
the acorn began to grow.